For children, and all the things you wonder. —B.J.

To Tim, a distant star and to Bisset, a gentle heart. The two brothers I love the best.—M.W.

Cover design by Vandy Ritter.
Book design by Ellen Toomey and Vandy Ritter.
Typeset in Goudy and Bernhard Modern.
Printed in Hong Kong.
The illustrations in this book were rendered in watercolor.

Library of Congress Information

Joosse, Barbara M.
I love you the purplest/ by Barbara M. Joosse; illustrated by Mary Whyte.
p. cm.
Summary: Two boys discover that their mother loves them equally but in different ways.
ISBN: 0-8118-0718-5
[1. Brothers–Fiction. 2. Mothers and sons–Fiction. 3. Fishing–Fiction.] I. Whyte, Mary, ill. II. Title.
PZ7.J7435Iae 1996
[Fic]–dc20 96-5221
CIP
AC

Distributed in Canada by Raincoast Books
8680 Cambie Street
Vancouver B.C. V6P 6M9

10 9 8 7 6 5 4

Chronicle Books
85 Second Street
San Francisco, CA 94105

Web Site: www.chronbooks.com

I Love You the Purplest

By Barbara M. Joosse
Illustrated by Mary Whyte

chronicle books · san francisco

Early in the evening
the brothers and their Mama
finished supper in the sturdy red cabin
and set out to fish.

The lake slowed its thrashing
to a soft, even beat.
The mosquitoes dipped low to the water
and the water bugs skittered on top.
The moon glowed on one side of the lake
while the sun shimmered on the other.
This was the time when fishing was best.

Max exploded from the cabin,
twirling the shovel in front of him.
Mama came next, and then Julian.
Julian shut the cabin door tightly
to keep it safe from burglars and bears.

Julian scooped the dirt
to find the fattest worms.

Max jumped on the shovel
and flung dirt in the air
until a tangle of worms filled his can.

“Mama, who has the most worms?” he asked.

Mama smiled.

“Max, your can is full of the liveliest worms.
And Julian, your can has the juiciest.”

Max, Julian and Mama stepped into the small wooden boat. Julian took one oar and Max took the other.

Julian planted his blue boots wide and took deep, even strokes. Max braced his red boots against the ribs of the boat and stroked quickly through the water.

The brothers' faces were hot and they gulped at the air. Julian gasped, "Mama, who's the best rower?"

Mama's eyes grew soft.
"Why, Julian, you took the deepest strokes.
And Max, your strokes were fastest."

The three fished until stars sprinkled the sky
and water turned dark as night. In the end,
Mama caught one fish, Julian caught one
fish and Max caught three.

“I’m the best fisherman,” cried Max, hoisting his fish in the air. Julian pushed his hat brim low on his face.

“Three fish! What a bountiful fisherman you are,” said Mama.

“And Julian, you’re the cleverest. Your fish hid in the weeds, but you waited. When your bobber jerked in the water you kept your pole high and you reeled in a fine, fat fish.”

When the fishing and the baths
and the stories were done,
Mama tucked the brothers into bed.

Julian slept in the top bunk
and she reached up to kiss him goodnight.

"Mama," whispered Julian,
his hands forming a tunnel around her ear.
"Who do you love best?"

Mama thought for a minute, and then she
whispered, "Why, Julian, I love you the bluest!
I love you the color of a dragon fly
at the tip of its wing.
I love you the color of a cave
in its deepest, hidden part
where grizzly bears and bats curl up until night.
The mist of a mountain.
The splash of a waterfall.
The hush of a whisper."

The breath in Julian's chest grew and grew
and grew until he couldn't hold it any longer.
Then it came out in a long, velvety sigh.

Mama crouched low to the bunk where Max slept.
Max wriggled his finger for Mama to come close.
He whispered, "Mama, who do you love best?"

"Why Max, I love you the reddest!
I love you the color of the sky
before it blazes into night.
I love you the color of a leopard's eyes
when it prowls through the jungle,
and the color of a campfire at the edge of the flame.
A wide open hug. The swirl of a magic cape.
The thunder of a shout."

The smile on Max's face grew and grew
until his cheeks couldn't hold it in.
Then it came out in a big, thundery laugh.

Later in the evening
the brothers and their Mama slept:
one in the top bunk,
glowing like the evening moon,
one in the bottom bunk,
shimmering like the evening sun,
and Mama in the big bed
dreaming of the boys she loved best.